A Note to Parents

For many children, learning math is difficult and "I hate math!" is their first response — to which many parents silently add "Me, too!" Children often see adults comfortably reading and writing, but they rarely have such models for mathematics. And math fear can be catching!

The easy-to-read stories in this *Hello Math* series were written to give children a positive introduction to mathematics and parents a pleasurable re-acquaintance with a subject that is important to everyone's life. *Hello Math* stories make mathematical ideas accessible, interesting, and fun for children. The activities and suggestions at the end of each book provide parents with a hands-on approach to help children develop mathematical interest and confidence.

Enjoy the mathematics!

• Give your child a chance to retell the story. The more familiar children are with the story, the more they will understand its mathematical concepts.
• Use the colorful illustrations to help children "hear and see" the math at work in the story.
• Treat the math activities as games to be played for fun. Follow your child's lead. Spend time on those activities that engage your child's interest and curiosity.
• Activities, especially ones using physical materials, help make abstract mathematical ideas concrete.

Learning is a messy process and learning about math calls for children to become immersed in lively experiences that help them make sense of mathematical concepts and symbols.

Although learning about numbers is basic to math, other ideas, such as identifying shapes and patterns, measuring, collecting and interpreting data, reasoning logically, and thinking about chance are also important. By reading these stories and having fun with the activities, you'll help your child enthusiastically say "*Hello, Math*," instead of "I hate math."

—Marilyn Burns
National Mathematics Educator
Author of *The I Hate Mathematics! Book*

To Sam
— G.M.

For Frank
—A.K.

Library of Congress Cataloging-in-Publication Data
Maccarone, Grace.
    The silly story of Goldie Locks and the three squares / by Grace
Maccarone ; illustrated by Anne Kennedy.
        p. cm. — (Hello math reader. Level 2)
    "Cartwheel Books."
    Summary: A modern descendant of the Goldilocks of folklore fame makes
a similar visit to a stranger's house — with a geometric twist.
    ISBN 0-590-54344-X
    [1. Shape — Fiction.] I. Kennedy, Anne 1955- ill. II. Title. III. Series.
PZ7.M1257Si 1996
[E] — dc20   95-13226
                                                                                   CIP
                                                                                    AC

12 11 10 9 8 7 6 5 4 3 2 1   6 7 8 9/9 0 1/0

Printed in the U.S.A.   23

First Scholastic printing, May 1996

The Silly Story of
Goldie Locks
and the
Three Squares

by Grace Maccarone
Illustrated by Anne Kennedy

Hello Math Reader — Level 2

SCHOLASTIC INC.
Cartwheel BOOKS®
New York Toronto London Auckland Sydney

This is a story
about a girl named Goldie Locks.
She isn't the Goldilocks
you know from the fairy tale.
The fairy-tale Goldilocks
lived long ago,
once upon a time.

The fairy-tale Goldilocks
is the great-great-grandmother
of our Goldie Locks.

Our Goldie Locks lives right now.
She is not at all
like her great-great-grandmother.
Or is she?

One day,
our Goldie Locks was walking
in the woods.
She saw a pretty house
in the shape of a pentagon.
It had five sides.

Goldie Locks was hungry
and tired, so she went into
the house.
It was stupid to walk
into a stranger's house
like that.

But that's what girls
named Goldie Locks
seem to do.

No one was home,
but there were three bowls
on the table.
The first bowl had noodles
that were shaped like triangles.

Some of the noodle triangles
had three equal sides.

Some of the noodle triangles
had two equal sides
and one different side.

Some of the noodle triangles
had three unequal sides.
None of the sides were the
same.

Yuck! Goldie Locks did not like
all these different triangles.

The noodles in the second bowl were shaped like rectangles.

Some noodle rectangles were long and skinny. Some noodle rectangles were short and wide.

Yuck! Goldie Locks did not like all these different rectangles.

The third bowl had
square noodles.
They were great!
All of the squares
had four equal sides.

Goldie Locks popped the
square noodles
into her round mouth.

Now Goldie Locks was no longer
hungry, but she was still tired.

She looked around.
She spotted three chairs
and tried them out.

The first chair was shaped
like a triangle. Goldie Locks
tried to sit on it. But she
could not. She fell on her
you-know-what. Ouch!

The second chair was shaped
like a circle.
As soon as Goldie Locks sat down,
the chair rolled away.

At first, that was fun.
Then Goldie Locks
fell on her you-know-what again.

Ouch! Ouch!

The third chair was shaped
like a rectangle.
It was just right—

until it broke.
Goldie Locks fell again.
Ouch! Ouch! Ouch!

Well, you know what
Goldie Locks saw next.
Right! Three beds.

Goldie Locks tried
the beds. One
was shaped
like a circle.
Goldie Locks
hated it.

Another bed was
shaped like a
triangle.

She hated that one, too.

The last bed was shaped like a
rectangle. It was just right,
and Goldie Locks fell asleep.

The Three Squares came home.
When they saw the big mess,
they knew they were not alone.
The Three Squares found Goldie
Locks asleep. They stared.
Goldie Locks woke up,
and she was scared.

But she still remembered this:
The shortest distance
between two points
is a straight line.

So Goldie Locks ran straight
out the door.
And she never circled back!

• ABOUT THE ACTIVITIES •

Before they enter school, children have a good deal of experience with geometric ideas from playing and building with shapes. During these early investigations, children begin to notice properties of shapes and develop ideas about them—round shapes roll, some shapes are pointy, these two go together and make one of those, etc. Young children also learn the names of some shapes: for example, square, rectangle, triangle, circle.

It's common, however, for children to have incomplete and sometimes incorrect ideas about shapes. For example, they think that triangles must always point up; to some children, a triangle in any other position is "upside down" or "sideways" and, therefore, somehow wrong. Or when some children see a square drawn on a tilt, they may call it a diamond and insist that it's not a square.

The activities in this section will engage your child in thinking more about shapes. These activities will also open up discussions about geometric ideas, and provide your child with experience linking correct mathematical vocabulary to geometric shapes. The directions are written for you to read along with your child. Follow your child's interests, and enjoy shape exploration!

— Marilyn Burns

> You'll find tips and suggestions
> for guiding the activities whenever
> you see a box like this!

Let's Trace Sides

Use the pictures from the book to find the shapes talked about in this activity.

When she was walking in the woods, Goldie Locks saw a house. "It had five sides," or was shaped like a pentagon. Trace the house to be sure it has five sides.

Inside the house, Goldie Locks found a bowl with noodles shaped like triangles. All of them had three sides. Use your finger to trace and check that the noodles have three sides.

The second bowl had noodles shaped like rectangles. Trace with your finger to be sure they have four sides.

Squares also have four sides. A square is a kind of rectangle. Trace the square noodles in the third bowl and count their sides.

The first chair Goldie Locks sat on was shaped like a triangle. Trace and count the chair's three sides.

Keep going through the book, tracing all the shapes and counting their sides.

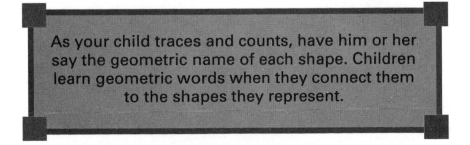

As your child traces and counts, have him or her say the geometric name of each shape. Children learn geometric words when they connect them to the shapes they represent.

Shape Hunt

What shapes do you see in this picture?

Can you find things inside or outside of your house that are shaped like triangles? Like squares and rectangles? Like circles? Like pentagons? Go on a shape hunt. See how many you can find.

Which shapes are easy to find? Which are hard to find?

Shape Pictures

Draw about 10 shapes on a sheet of paper. Be sure to include at least one of each of these shapes: triangle, rectangle, square, pentagon, and circle.

Color the shapes different colors and cut them out. Then arrange some or all of them on another piece of paper to make a shape picture. Paste them down.

Show your picture to others. See if they can name the shapes you made.

Things to Think About

Things shaped like circles roll, but things shaped like squares don't. Why do you think this is so?

Rectangles can be long and skinny or short and wide. (Look at the noodles in the bowls.) But squares, whether they're large or small, always have the same shape. Why do you think this is so?

Goldie Locks liked the bed that looked like a rectangle, but she didn't like the ones that looked like a circle and a triangle. Which do you think is the best shape for a bed? Why?

At the end of the story, Goldie Locks remembered that "the shortest distance between two points is a straight line." Can you explain why that's the shortest distance?

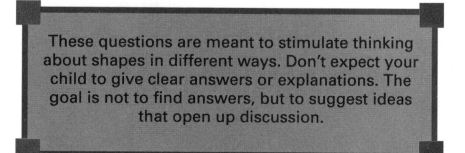

These questions are meant to stimulate thinking about shapes in different ways. Don't expect your child to give clear answers or explanations. The goal is not to find answers, but to suggest ideas that open up discussion.